Martha of California

A Story of the California Trail

JAMES OTIS

Copyright © 2016
Edited By EriK Publications
All rights reserved.

ISBN-13: 978-1532920318
ISBN-10: 1532920318

FOREWORD

The author of this series of stories for children has endeavored simply to show why and how the descendants of the early colonists fought their way through the wilderness in search of new homes. The several narratives deal with the struggles of those adventurous people who forced their way westward, ever westward, whether in hope of gain or in answer to "the call of the wild," and who, in so doing, wrote their names with their blood across this country of ours from the Ohio to the Columbia.

To excite in the hearts of the young people of this land a desire to know more regarding the building up of this great nation, and at the same time to entertain in such a manner as may stimulate to noble deeds, is the real aim of these stories. In them there is nothing of romance, but only a careful, truthful record of the part played by children in the great battles with those forces, human as well as natural, which, for so long a time, held a vast portion of this broad land against the advance of home seekers.

With the knowledge of what has been done by our own people in our own land, surely there is no reason why one should resort to fiction in order to depict scenes of heroism, daring, and sublime disregard of suffering in nearly every form.

JAMES OTIS.

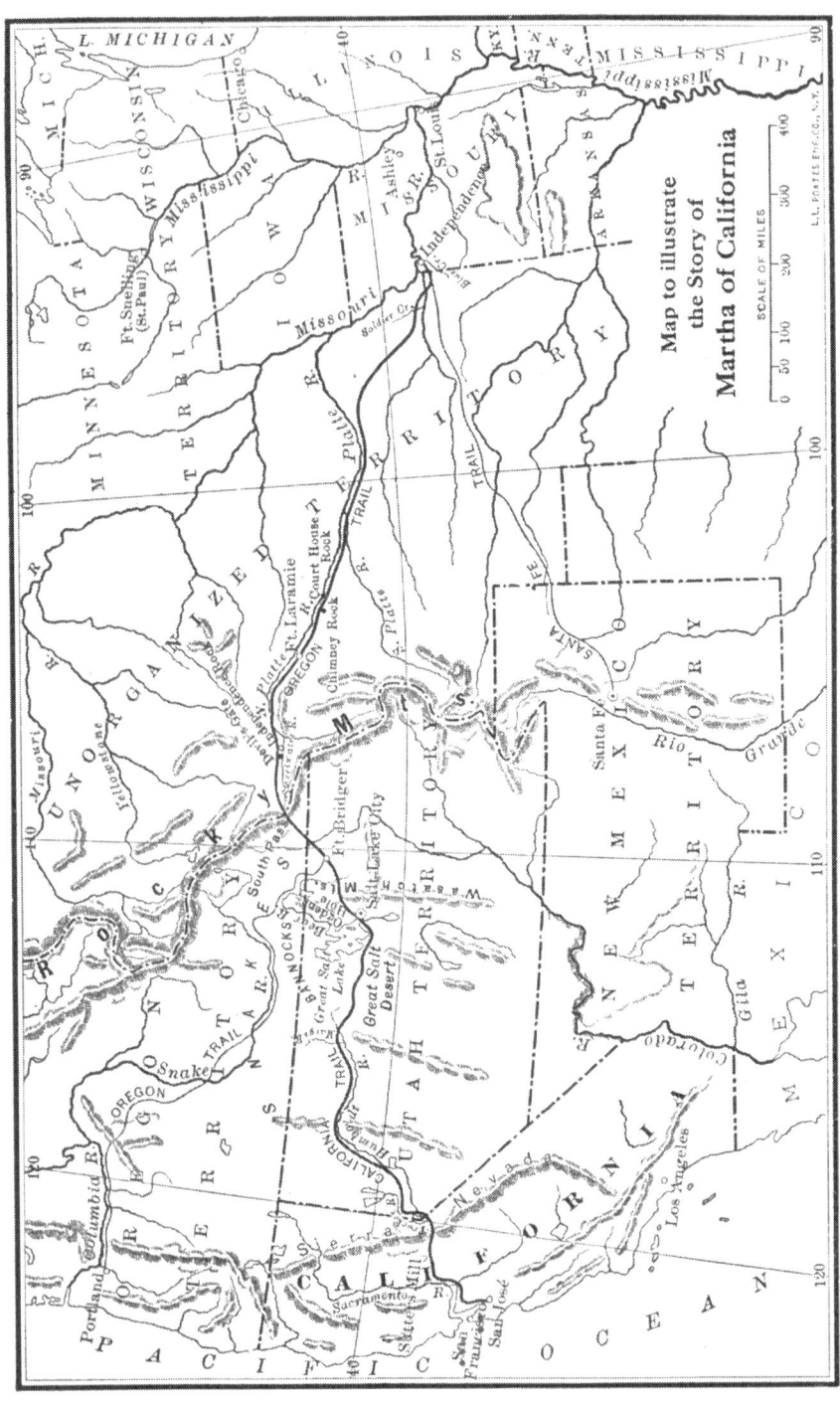

Map to illustrate the Story of Martha of California

A CHANGE OF HOMES

In case one should ask in the years to come how it happened that I, Martha Early, who was born in Ashley, Pike County, in the state of Missouri, and lived there until I was twelve years old, journeyed across the prairies and deserts to California, the question can be answered if I write down what I saw when so many people from our county went to make new homes in that state where gold had been found in such abundance.

For my part, I used to wonder why people should be willing to leave Missouri, enduring the many hardships they knew awaited them on the journey of two thousand miles, in order to buy land in a country where nearly all the inhabitants were Spaniards and Mexicans.

I suppose the stories told about the wonderful quantity of gold which had suddenly been found in California caused our people to think particularly of that far-off land. When the excitement of getting rich by digging in the earth a few weeks or a few months had in a measure died away, there came tales regarding the fertile soil and the beauty of the country, until nearly every one in Pike County, as well as in the county of the same name just across the Mississippi River in the state of Illinois, much the same as had a fever for moving.

Perhaps that is why the people we met while journeying called all the emigrants "Pikers." You see there were so many from both the Pike counties who went into California in the year 1851, that it appeared to strangers as if every person on the trail had come from Pike County.

"JOE BOWERS"

Then, too, fully half of all these emigrants were singing or whistling that song of "Joe Bowers," which was supposed to have been written by a Piker, and to represent a man from Missouri or Illinois.

Surely every one remembers it. The first verse, and if I have heard it once I certainly have a thousand times, goes like this:—

> "My name it is Joe Bowers
> And I've got a brother Ike.
> I came from old Missouri,
> Yes, all the way from Pike."

The song was intended to show that this Joe Bowers came from our county, and, perhaps, because so many of the emigrants were singing it, all of us who went into California in the year 1851 were, as I have said, called "Pikers."

However the name came about, I was a Piker, and before we arrived in this wondrously beautiful country, I wished again and again that I had been almost any other than an emigrant, for the way was long, and

oh! so wearisome.

I must always think of Missouri as being one of the best of all the states in the Union, because it was there I was born and there I went to school until father caught the California fever, which resulted in our setting out on a journey which, for a time, seemed endless.

My father had no idea of going so far simply to dig for gold. He had seen many who went across the country in 1849 believing they would come back rich as kings, yet who returned home poorer in pocket than when they left; therefore he came to understand that only a few of all that vast army of miners who hastened into California after the discovery at Sutter's Mill, got enough of the precious metal to pay for the food they ate.

Father thought he could buy better land in California than was to be found in Pike County, for to have heard the stories told by some of the people who had come back disappointed from the land of gold, you might have believed that one had only to put a few seeds at random in the ground in order to gather marvelous crops.

THE REASONS FOR MOVING

Nor was my father the only man who put faith in at least some of the fanciful tales told concerning the land of California which had so lately been given up to the United States by the Spaniards. Our neighbors for miles around were in a state of unrest and excitement, until it was decided that nearly all would undertake the long journey, and I could not prevent myself from wondering if Pike County would not feel lonely to have the people abandon it, for it surely seemed as if every man, woman, and child was making haste to leave Missouri in search of the wondrous farming lands.

Mother looked woefully solemn when, on a certain evening, father came home and told us that he had sold the plantation for about half as much as it had cost him, and was going to join the next company that set out from Pike County.

It was a long time before mother would have very much to say about the journey, but as the days passed and the neighbors who were going with us came to our home that they might talk over the preparations for moving, she became interested in making plans, although again and again, when we two were alone, she told me that this trailing over two thousand miles of deserts and mountains was not to her liking.

MOTHER'S ANXIETY

It was only natural she should be worried about making such a great change, for all father's worldly goods consisted of the Pike County plantation and the live stock, and if, after selling the land and spending very nearly all his money to provide for the journey, we found that California farms were no better than the one we were leaving, it would be the saddest kind of mistake.

"Your father has set his mind on going; the homestead has been sold, and we must make the best of it, Martha, hoping that half the stories we have heard about California are true," she said to me so many times that I came almost to believe it was a foolish venture upon which we were about to embark.

Then, when I began to wonder how we were to live during such a long journey, and asked mother if it would be possible for us to cook and churn and do the family washing while traveling in an ox wagon, she would say with a sigh:—

"Don't, Martha, don't ask questions that I can't answer! It seems to me almost certain that we shall starve to death before getting anywhere near California, even if we are not killed by Indians or wild beasts, without having had time to get very hungry or dirty."

Yet we did travel the two thousand miles, walking the greater part of the way, and although there were many times when all of us were hungry, none actually starved to death; nor were we killed by wild beasts or Indians, else I could not be here in this beautiful place writing this story.

Father spent days and days getting ready for the moving. After he had finished the preparations, I thought the journey would not be so terribly hard, because he had arranged everything so snug and cozy for mother and me, that it really seemed as if we might take actual comfort in case we could make shift to do housework in a wagon.

HOW WE WERE TO TRAVEL

We owned only four yoke of cattle, but with some of the money received from the sale of the plantation, we bought as many more, which gave us sixteen oxen. We were to take with us all five of the cows and both the horses, on which father said mother and I might ride when we were tired of sitting in the wagon; but I knew what kind of animals ours were under the saddle, and said to myself that it would be many a long day before I would trust myself on the back of either.

It would have done you good to see our movable home after father had made it ready, and by that I mean the wagon in which mother and I were to ride. It was small compared with the other, in which were to be carried enough furniture for a single room, farming tools, grain for the cattle, and a host of things; but I did not give much heed to the load because I was so deeply interested in what was to be a home for mother and me during many a month.

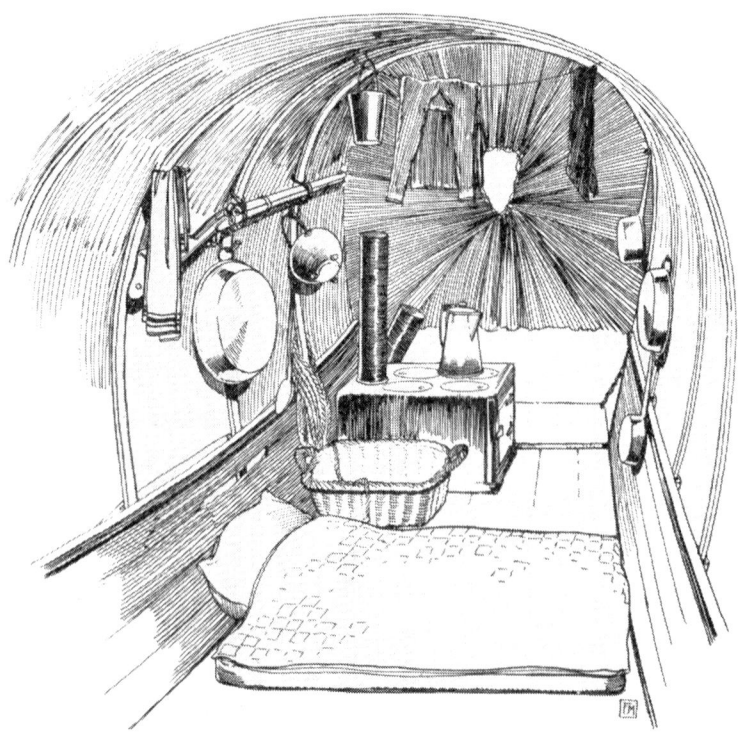

That wagon was enough to attract the attention of any girl, for, fitted up as I first saw it, the inside looked really like a playhouse, and when I said as much to father, he declared that I was indeed the right kind of girl to go into a wild country, if I could find anything like sport during the tramp from Pike County to California.

I surely must tell you about that wagon before setting down anything concerning the journey. It was what is known as a Conestoga, and one may see many of the same kind on the Santa Fe or the Oregon trail. Imagine a boxlike cart nearly as long as an ordinary bedroom and so wide that I could stretch myself out at full length across the body. The top and sides were covered with osnaburg sheeting, which is cloth made of flax or tow. Some people really sleep between sheets made of that coarse stuff, but it is so rough and irritating to the flesh that I had far rather lie on the floor than in a bed where it is used.

Osnaburg sheeting makes excellent wagon covers, however, for the rain cannot soak through the cloth, and it is so cheap that one can well afford to use it in double thickness, which serves to keep out the wind as well as the water.

OUR MOVABLE HOME

The front of the wagon and a small window-like place at the end were left open, but could be securely closed with curtains that buttoned at the sides.

Around the inside of the wagon were hung such things as we might need to use often during the journey. There were pots and pans, towels, clothing, baskets, and two rifles, for father believed weapons might be required when we came upon disagreeable savages, or if game was to be found within shooting distance.

Our cookstove was set up at the rear end of the wagon, where it could be pushed out on a small shelf fastened to the rear axle, when we wanted to use it. A most ingenious contrivance we found that shelf to be, for mother and I could remain inside the wagon and do our cooking in stormy weather; but those women of the company whose husbands had not been so thoughtful were forced to stay out of doors while preparing a meal, no matter how hard it might be raining.

Our beds were laid in the bottom of the wagon and covered with the bedclothes to save them from being badly soiled, as would be likely if we slept upon them at night, and cooked, ate, and did the housework on them during the daytime.

We did not try to carry many dishes, because there were so many chances they would be broken, but nearly everything of the kind we used was of metal, such as tin or iron.

Underneath the cart were hung buckets, the churn, lanterns, and such a collection of articles that I could not but fancy people might believe we were peddlers carrying so large an assortment of goods that they had overrun the wagon body.

What puzzled me before we started on the journey was how we could persuade the cows to travel as we would have them; but I soon came to understand that it was a simple matter.

LEAVING ASHLEY

You must know that father was not the only man in Ashley that intended to build up a new home in California. More than half of the people were making preparations for the journey, and when we finally set off the procession was very imposing, with more than fifty wagons, not one of them drawn by less than three yoke of oxen or four pairs of mules; there were cows almost without number and a flock of thirty or forty sheep.

I said to myself then, that we need have no fear the savages would try to make trouble for us, because when they saw so many people, the poor, ignorant things would believe everybody on the banks of the Mississippi was heading for California, and it would be a very brave Indian who dared be other than polite to such a large company.

Even though you had never before heard of Pike County, it would have been most interesting to see the people of Ashley on the morning we set off. As Ellen Morgan, a particular friend of mine who was going to California also, said to me just before we drove away, "It is much as if all the folks in the world had come to see us leave town."

The streets were actually thronged, as I have heard it said the streets of a large city oftentimes are, and what with the shouts of the men, the screams of the children, and the lowing of the cattle, it was quite as much as I could do to make myself heard when I tried to tell Ellen that at the last minute mother had given permission for her to ride in our wagon.

Of course the noise in the street could not have been as great as I fancied, for Ellen had no trouble in hearing me, as was shown when

she came running back to our wagon with her Sunday frock and other valuable things neatly done up in a corn sack.

Then it seemed to me that no improvement could be made upon our manner of traveling, for we two girls were to be together all the while, and even when the weather was stormy, it would seem really cozy under our double thickness of osnaburg cloth.

It surprised me very much because mother acted as if it saddened her to set off on what could not fail to be a delightful journey. I saw tears in her eyes when she came out of our old home for the last time, and wondered if she was sorry because she was leaving the house where we had lived so long, or whether she believed we would never find another such delightful town as Ashley.

Of course I felt just a little tearful when those people who were to remain at home gathered around the wagon to say "good-by"; but there were so many of our neighbors in the company we would not have a chance to be lonely, and I was certain that all the friends we were leaving behind would soon join us, having come to realize, as had father, that California was the only proper place in which to live.

EBEN JORDAN

If I could have had everything arranged exactly to please me, I would have insisted that Eben Jordan be left in Ashley. He is a boy about six months older than I, who always seems to take the greatest delight in teasing us girls. I had no doubt but that he would be very disagreeable at times, and felt, on that first day, as if there could be no cloud on the California skies if Eben had remained in Pike County.

It is no more than fair for me to say, however, that, much as I disliked the boy, Eben Jordan was one who ever kept his ears open to the conversation of his elders and was more than willing to repeat to Ellen and me whatever he learned.

Even before our company had left Ashley, he told us the journey was to be begun by first going to Independence, a town on the Missouri River where the Santa Fe traders and those who would journey by the Oregon trail made ready for the long march.

Up to this time I had had no idea of how we were to get to California, save we drove directly across the prairies and over the mountains, always in a westerly direction.

But I must have understood that we could not strike off across the country in any direction we fancied, because we must follow some trail in order to find a plentiful supply of grass for the cattle and mules and sheep, as well as water for ourselves.

Eben said that the leaders of the company, among whom was my father, had talked not a little regarding the country through which we should pass. Thus he learned that we would journey over what is known as the Oregon trail as far as Fort Bridger, after which, striking off to the southward somewhat, we would go along the shores of the Great Salt Lake, past Ogden's Hole, to the land of the Bannock Indians. Then the course was to be as nearly westward as the foothills

would permit.

"It will be a rare time for us all," Eben said gleefully, after having told us girls that we would journey nearly two thousand miles before coming to that land for which we sought. "There will be game until a fellow can't rest, and after we are once well on the way, we shall come upon Indian tribe after Indian tribe, when you girls will be only too glad to shelter yourselves under my wing, for there is no knowing what the savages may take it into their heads to do, providing the opportunity offers."

Ellen was not a little displeased because Eben seemingly believed we would be glad of his protection, and I really felt uneasy in mind when the lad left us to go to his father's wagon, saying:—

"It isn't well for you girls to be so high and mighty, because before this journey has come to an end you may be glad that I am willing to lend a hand."

Ellen laughed at the idea that the time would ever come when we might accept a favor from Eben Jordan. She seemed so certain nothing disagreeable could happen to us while our company was so large, that I soon put away all forebodings and gave strict attention to what was before us.

ON THE ROAD

It had taken our fathers considerable time to get the people and the cattle in proper marching order; but once this was done, they gave the word for the procession to move forward, and the people at Ashley whom we were leaving behind cheered us wildly as we went slowly out from the town.

It seemed much like taking part in some wondrous celebration, to be riding thus amid those who were cheering and, I dare say, envying us.

Mother was content to sit inside the wagon, where father had placed a short-legged chair for her convenience, but Ellen and I remained on the front seat where we could see all that was going on, and until we were

well clear of the town it did seem to me that I was a very important person.

It was late in the forenoon before we started, therefore no halt was to be made for dinner, but this gave me little uneasiness, for mother had an ample supply of cooked provisions on hand.

Our neighbors at Ashley had spoken again and again of the hardships which we would encounter before arriving at the shores of the Pacific Ocean, and I said to Ellen, when we were two or three miles from the town, that I could not understand how any one could believe such a journey might be either wearisome or dangerous.

EBEN'S PREDICTIONS

Surely we were as comfortable as two girls could be, with a covering over our heads in case it rained, and enough food to satisfy our desires.

Therefore what difference did it make, as I said to Ellen, whether we were five months or six on the march? Eben Jordan, who had come back from his father's wagon along the line of procession as if to see that everything was right, overhearing my words, replied with a laugh, which sounded to me very disagreeable:—

"You may well say, Martha Early, that this portion of the journey is easy. We are now traveling on a beaten road, with nothing to prevent our going forward at the best pace of the oxen. Wait until we have really started, after having come to Independence, and leave the highway to take to the trail. You will find the wagon tumbling and pitching over the rocks, or floundering across fords, where watch must be kept sharply against the Indians, and every man needs to have his eyes open lest he be attacked by wild beasts. Then you shall say to me whether it makes no difference to you if this journey requires five months or six."

I refused to listen to the lad, who seemed to find the greatest pleasure in making other people uncomfortable in mind, and I turned toward Ellen, as if speaking to her very earnestly in whispers, thereby causing Eben to believe I had not heard what he said, whereupon he went off laughing.

WHAT WE HEARD ABOUT CALIFORNIA

We had heard people talking about the wonderful fortunes to be found in California, until it seemed as if we might become rich simply by digging in the ground a bit; but, as you shall hear, before our journey had come to an end we understood that however much valuable metal there might be in the earth, it was not to be gathered like pebbles.

We met on our way hundreds of people who had gone into California with great expectations and were coming back poorer than when they set out; but on the first day we were ignorant of all this, and quite convinced that it was a simple matter to become wealthy by a very little labor.

Before night came there was to me less pleasure than during the first hour or two. The wagon jolted over the roads roughly, making it necessary to hold firmly to the seat, lest I be thrown off, and it became wearisome to sit so long in one position.

Mother, who stretched herself out upon a bed in the bottom of the wagon when she was tired of sitting upright, did not weary so soon of this kind of traveling; but nevertheless she was quite as well pleased as

Ellen and I, when, about four o'clock in the afternoon, word was given that we should halt and make camp.

THE FIRST ENCAMPMENT

We were yet in a fairly thickly settled portion of the country; but the leaders of our company determined to make the encampment exactly as if we were on the prairie or among the mountains, where there might be danger from wild beasts or wilder savages, and you may well fancy that Ellen and I were on our feet as soon as the wagon came to a stop, for we had heard so much of this camp making that both of us were eager to see how it was done.

All the wagons were drawn up in a large circle so that the tongue of one came close to the tailboard of another, and just inside this ring of vehicles were set up small tents, which many of the company were to use at night because their families were so large that every one could not be given room in the wagons.

Inside this row of tents were picketed the horses, or, at least, they were to be picketed as soon as night should come; but when we first halted they were fastened out upon the plain where they might eat the grass, while the oxen, cows, and sheep were turned loose with half a dozen of the men and boys watching lest they should stray.

Because the people were not accustomed to thus making an encampment, no little time was spent in getting everything into what the leaders of the company believed to be proper order, and then our mothers set about cooking supper.

In our wagon the stove was pushed back upon the shelf made expressly for it, short lengths of pipe were run through the osnaburg cloth and tied by wire to the topmost part of the rear wagon bow, so they might be held straight, and then mother set about her work much as if she had been at home.

It was most pleasant camping in the open air, and before we had been halted an hour the place was quite homelike.

At nearly every wagon one or more women were making ready for supper; a short distance away the men and the boys were herding the cattle, and near by, inside or out of the inclosure, were scores and scores of idle ones, who, their work being done, were now enjoying a time of rest.

There was much talking and shouting, but above all one could hear that song of the true Pikers:—

> "My name it is Joe Bowers,
> And I've got a brother Ike.
> I came from old Missouri,
> Yes, all the way from Pike."

NIGHT IN CAMP

How Ellen and I enjoyed the supper on this first night of the journey! Mother made sour-milk biscuit; the stove worked to perfection, as if delighted because it was being carried to California; and what with cold meat and steaming hot tea it seemed as if I had never tasted anything better than that meal.

Although we had enjoyed ourselves hugely, especially during the first part of the day's march, both Ellen and I were tired, and when mother said we might make up our bed on the bottom of the wagon, we were not only willing, but eager to do so, for after the hearty supper it seemed as if sleep had become a necessity.

Once we had crossed over into Dreamland, our eyes were not opened again until the sun was near to rising; then the shouts of the men and the lowing of the cattle caused us to spring up suddenly, almost fancying that the camp had been attacked by savages, even though we were not yet out of Pike County.

If I had the time, it would please me to describe the journey from our home in Ashley to a town known as Independence, on the Missouri River, where the Oregon trail begins; but since, as father said again and again, we did not really start until we had struck the Oregon trail, it is best that I leave out all that happened while we were coming from Pike County to the Missouri River.

THE TOWN OF INDEPENDENCE

We traveled slowly, because the cows were not easily herded, and, as Eben Jordan said, none of our people were accustomed to such kind of marching.

We did, however, finally arrive at the real starting point after eight days, during which time Ellen and I came to understand that, however pleasant it was to sit in the wagon and look out upon the country through which we passed, it might grow wearisome.

Ellen and I had fancied we would see something very new and wonderful at Independence, and yet, while everything was strange and there was much to attract one's attention, it was not so very different from other settlements through which we had passed.

There was, however, a constant bustle and confusion such as one could not see elsewhere. Enormous wagons, which Eben Jordan said belonged to the traders who went over the Santa Fe trail, were coming into town or going out, each drawn by eight or ten mules and accompanied by Spaniards or Negroes, until one could but wonder where so

many people were going.

There were trains, much like our own, belonging to settlers who were going into Oregon, or, like ourselves, into California. Those were halted just outside the town, until the entire settlement was literally surrounded, while among them all, near the wagons of the traders as well as those of the emigrants, lounged Indians, nothing like the people I had imagined the savages to be.

KANSAS INDIANS

As Ellen said, if that was the kind of Indian we should meet with during the journey, then we need have little or no fear, for the savages we saw at Independence were nothing more nor less than beggars, who would greedily pick up and devour anything eatable that was thrown at them. Eben

Jordan made himself ridiculous by marching around armed with a rifle, and a huge knife thrust in his belt, as if expecting each instant to be called upon to defend his life.

We were tired of the settlement, even before we had fairly arrived,  and after Ellen and I walked through the town, wondering not a little at seeing a number of the houses and stores built entirely of brick, we were content to return to our own encampment, which was about half a mile out on the prairie.

LOOKING INTO THE FUTURE FOR TROUBLE

Up to this time mother and I had but little trouble in preparing the meals whenever we came to a halt; but I heard some of the men say that within a few days after we were once on the trail, all this would be changed. There would be many times when we might not find sufficient fuel to keep a fire in the stove, when we would feel the pangs of thirst because of not being able to get enough water, and when, the stock of provisions which we had brought with us having been consumed, we would know what it was to be hungry.

When I repeated to mother what I had heard, she nodded her head sadly, replying that she had thought of all these things when father first determined to seek a new home in the California country, and she doubted not that we would come to know much suffering, before we arrived at our journey's end.

As may be supposed, I was not in a cheerful mood when Ellen and I went to bed that night. During the half hour or more while we lay there wakeful, we spoke of all the possibilities of the future, and almost regretted that our parents had decided to leave Pike County, for surely they could find nowhere on the face of this earth a place more agreeable in which to live.

A STORMY DAY

When another morning came, it surely seemed as if all my fears were about to be realized, for the day dawned dark and forbidding, the rain came down in torrents, while the wind sighed and moaned as it drove floods of water from one end of the wagon to the other, wetting us completely even before we were awake.

I could not believe father would set off on the journey at such a time as this, and was wondering how we should be able to cook breakfast, when he called to mother that she make ready the morning meal, for in half an hour the train would be in motion.

No one had been sufficiently thoughtful to store beneath the wagon

a supply of dry fuel, and the consequence was that we had nothing with which to build a fire, save a few armfuls of water-soaked wood which father and Eben Jordan succeeded in gathering, for where so many emigrants were encamped, fuel of any kind was indeed scarce.

I almost forgave Eben for having appeared so ridiculous when he strutted around fully armed, as I saw him striving to gather wood for us when he might have remained under the cover of his father's wagon; indeed, before many days passed both Ellen and I saw that there was much good in the boy's heart, even though he was too often disposed to make matters disagreeable for us girls.

A LACK OF FUEL

Mother and I made our first attempt at cooking while the stove was beneath the wagon cover and the pipe thrust out through the hole in the rear.

If we had had plenty of dry wood, I have no doubt but that the work could have been done with some degree of comfort; but as it was, we were put to our wits' ends, even to get sufficient heat to boil the water, and when word was given for the company to start, we had not really begun to cook the breakfast.

Of course it would have been dangerous for us to attempt to keep a fire burning while the wagon was moving. Therefore we would have been forced to set off without breakfast, had not Ellen's mother kindly sent us some corn bread which she had baked the night before, and this, with fresh milk, made up our meal.

At the time I thought I was much injured because of not having more food; but before we had come to the land of California I often looked back upon that morning with longing, remembering the meal of corn bread and milk as though it was a feast.

During all the long day, except for half an hour at noon, the patient oxen plodded wearily on amid the rain, oftentimes sinking fetlock-deep in the marshy places. Everything was damp and every place uncomfortable, and at times it seemed as if I could no longer bear up under the suffering.

In order to teach me that, instead of grumbling, I ought to be thankful for the comforts I could enjoy, mother told me to look at those who were exposed to the storm. I saw father and the other men walking beside the oxen, the rain pelting down upon them pitilessly; I heard the cry of a baby in pain; and I soon came to understand that my lot was far less hard than that of many others.

She read me a lesson on patience and contentment, whatever might be my surroundings, until I grew ashamed of having shown myself so disagreeable.

MAKING CAMP IN A STORM

Determined as I was to make the best of whatever might happen, I could not but be disheartened when, nearly at nightfall, we halted to make camp again. The rain was still descending like a cloud-burst; everything around us, including the bedding, seemed saturated with water. Yet I saw the men spread the thin cloth tents, after the wagons had been drawn up in a circle, or made into a corral as the travelers on the trail call it; I saw them wade ankle-deep in the mud, but with never

an impatient word or gesture. It appeared sufficient to them if their women and children could enjoy some little degree of comfort.

Again we strove to do our cooking under the wagon covers, and again we were in need of fuel. Ellen and I, with the skirts of our gowns over our heads for protection, scurried here and there, picking up twigs and crying out with delight when we came upon a piece of wood as large as one's fist.

You can well imagine what kind of supper we had that night. The inside of the wagon was filled with smoke, for the short length of stovepipe did not afford a strong draft, and mother labored, with the tears streaming down her cheeks, to fry as much bacon as would satisfy our hunger.

The smoke was so dense that we all wept, smiling even in the midst of our seeming tears when father said, after he had milked the cows and had brought in quite as much water as milk, that it was a question with him whether he could stand better the smoke or the rain. He was inclined to think he had rather be soaked with water than cured like a ham.

Again Eben Jordan showed his kindness of heart, for he insisted upon helping this man and that, milk the cows and herd the oxen and sheep, and he did whatever came to his hand, all the while humming "Joe Bowers."

When Eben came into our wagon later in the evening, Ellen and I treated him very kindly, for we were coming to understand that this boy, who found so much pleasure in vexing us girls, was ever ready to do a good turn to another, even when it cost him much labor and discomfort.

A THUNDERSTORM

During all that night it rained; but shortly after midnight there came up such a terrific storm of thunder and lightning that it seemed as if the very heavens were bursting.

Then all our men and boys were forced to go and quiet the cattle, for the beasts were even as frightened as we girls were, and, so father said, would have stampeded, leaving us to spend the next day searching for them on the prairies, had it not been for the precautions of our people.

When I complained to mother, just after father had gone out into the tempest, that this journey to California was nothing like what I had

pictured it, she said mildly that if I was growing disheartened now, it would have been better had I never set out from Pike County, for thus far matters had gone much to our convenience and that shortly we would find real trials and real troubles.

Next morning, however, my spirits rose, for the sun was shining brightly when I awoke; but word was passed around the camp that instead of setting off at once, we might spend two hours drying the bed clothing and such of our belongings as had been saturated during the storm.

Then there was presented such a scene as would have interested any one who had never witnessed the like before. On every wagon tongue were hung blankets and garments of all kinds, and over the wheels of each cart lay feather beds or bolsters, until it must have looked as if every member of our company had spent a day in washing, and was now about to do the ironing.

Eben Jordan went here and there, aiding this one or that when he had done what he might for his mother, all the while singing "My name it is Joe Bowers," until, even before our breakfast had been cooked, fully half the company were joining in that foolish song. Mother said almost fretfully, when Ellen and I took up the refrain, that she wished the senseless words had never been written, or that we had never heard them.

ANOTHER COMPANY OF PIKERS

Although we started off late that morning, owing to the drying out, we halted early in the afternoon, for we had come upon a company of men and women who, like ourselves, were bound for the land of California. The leader of the company was Colonel Russell.

To my surprise and delight these people also proved to be Pikers, having come from a settlement about twenty miles south of our old home.

You may readily fancy how enjoyable was that evening, when we visited from wagon to wagon, listening to the stories of what had thus far happened to the company, and repeating our own adventures, if such they could be called.

While we women and girls were thus engaged, the men of both companies decided to travel together, believing that by increasing the number there might be less danger from the Indians, for Eben Jordan said that the savages we saw at Independence were but imitations of the fiercer ones whom we were most likely to meet before our journey's end.

THE STOCK STRAY AWAY

I suppose it was the excitement occasioned by the meeting with Colonel Russell's company, which caused our men in charge of the cattle to be careless during the evening and later in the night, for when morning came we found that nearly all the oxen and a goodly number of the cows had strayed from the camp and disappeared completely.

When Eben Jordan first told us of this, I believed a great disaster had come upon us; but straightway father and half a dozen of the other men mounted the horses and set off across the prairie in search of the missing cattle, as if this was trouble to be expected.

In fact, before many days passed, I came to look upon the straying or the stampeding of the live stock as of little consequence.

We had plenty of time to cook breakfast that morning while the men

were searching over the prairie for the cattle, and, much to my surprise, within three hours all the stock had been brought into the encampment and we were making ready once more for the day's journey.

Before noon we arrived at Blue Creek, where we had, as it seemed to me, much trouble because the trail leading to the stream was deep with mud, and the bottom of the creek so soft that our people were forced to wade waist-deep on either side of the wagons, lest the wheels sink so far down that the oxen would not be able to pull the heavy loads across.

Again and again the men laid hold of the wheels, straining every muscle as the drivers of the cattle urged the patient beasts to their utmost exertions, and before all our company had crossed that small creek the day was so nearly at an end that there was nothing left for us to do save camp once more, although we had traveled only six miles since setting out.

Then came Sunday morning, when I believed we would remain idle, for it did not seem right that we should travel on the Lord's day; but, as father said, while we were making such a long journey it was necessary to push ahead during every hour of fair weather, and to take our day of rest only when it was absolutely necessary.

And so, instead of worshiping God as we would have done had we remained in Pike County, we went forward, fording two small creeks and journeying over a dull, level plain, whereon, save flowers, nothing was to be seen to delight the eye.

AN INDIAN VILLAGE

Within an hour of sunset we came to a veritable Indian village, although there were not many of the savages living in it, and Ellen and I took advantage of this first opportunity to see the redskins in their homes.

There were but four men, with perhaps a dozen women and children, all living in lodges made of smoke-dried skins, and looking exceedingly

dirty and disagreeable.

We girls were not inclined to linger there long, although the Indians were willing we should, and when our short visit had been brought to a close, they followed us, clustering around our wagons and waiting patiently for food to be thrown to them.

From this time on during a full week we continued to push steadily forward, moving so slowly that even we girls could understand the journey would be exceedingly long and wearisome.

I WEARY WITH SO MUCH TRAVELING

More than once did I reproach myself with having been so eager to leave Pike County, and many times I said to myself that a girl who has a happy home is indeed foolish to wish for a change, lest, like Ellen and me, they find, as mother often says, that they have jumped out of the frying pan into the fire.

One day was much like another. Now the trail would be hard

underfoot and the traveling easy, and again we would cross a stream, the bottom lands of which were so marshy that the oxen lugged and strained at their yokes, until oftentimes it was necessary to double up the teams in order that the heavy wagons could be pulled over the soft footing.

The only thing I remember which came to break the monotony of the slow march was when, on a certain evening, father returned with his pockets and hands full of wild onions which he had found on the prairie. Because our meals had consisted chiefly of corn bread and salted meat, I said to myself that now we would have a feast.

But alas! those wild onions were like my dreams about traveling to the land of California. While they looked fair on the outside before being cooked, they were so strong to the taste that one nearly choked in trying to eat them.

EBEN'S BOASTS

Eben Jordan, hearing of my disappointment, said with a laugh that when we came to the country where game was to be found he intended to bring into camp all the fresh meat the company could eat, and one might have thought from the way the boy talked that he believed himself capable of feeding all our company unaided.

It would have been well if Eben had contented himself with predicting the marvels which he counted on performing; but, instead, he reminded me that before we had come into the Land of Promise I might be more than willing to eat wild onions and "smack my lips over the disagreeable food."

It seems that he heard, while in Independence, of the sufferings of some people who had journeyed over that same trail, when they found no game and their provisions were consumed before the march came to an end.

It would have been better, so I said to him, if he had not repeated such things, for surely we were getting all the discomfort that was needed to show how foolish we had been in leaving Pike County, where no one suffered from hunger or thirst, if he had a tongue in his head to make known his desires.

It seemed almost as if the boy was a real prophet, for within a few hours Ellen and I did come to know what thirst—bitter, parching thirst—was like.

We had started out one morning when the rays of the sun beat down upon us so fervently that the wagon covering seemed to be no protection, and the only relief we had was from the gentle breeze which was blowing, not with sufficient force to relieve our suffering, but enough to prevent us from being literally baked.

SUFFERING WITH THIRST

We drank, as did all our company, of the water which we carried in kegs stowed in the wagons, and gave no heed to the fact that the supply was scanty, for until this time there had never been any lack of water.

At noon even the breeze died away; there was not a cloud in the sky, the trail was smooth and hard, running over what father called the tableland of the prairie, and the heat so intense that there were times when it surely seemed as if I could not longer continue to breathe.

Then, when our sufferings were seemingly as great as they could possibly be, mother discovered that our store of water had been exhausted, and called to father, asking that he get a supply from one of the other wagons.

It seemed strange to me then, and does even now, that at almost the same time all our company had run short of water, and from one end of the long train to the other we could not beg enough to moisten our tongues.

Perhaps it was the knowledge that I could not quench my thirst which caused me to suffer more severely, and when father said we must travel no less than twelve miles before coming to any stream, my heart sank within me.

Ellen was suffering quite as much as I, except that she had the good sense to hold her peace, and mother, patient with me as ever, said all she could to prevent me from dwelling too much upon my condition.

Nor was I the only one in that company to suffer severely. Whenever the train came to a halt that the cattle might have a breathing spell, I could hear the smaller children crying for something to drink, and once during the afternoon Eben Jordan came alongside our wagon, asking if our water kegs were empty.

Then I saw upon his face that look of eagerness and desire such as I had read on Ellen's, and when I told him we were suffering from thirst even more than any other members of the company, he shook his head and replied:—

"It is the younger ones who suffer the most, Martha Early, for they cannot be made to understand that it is necessary to wait; while you and I, who are older, know it is only a case of grinning and bearing it as best we may."

IN SEARCH OF WATER

I was irritated because Eben should read me a lesson, for indeed his words sounded like a reproof. I turned away from him, saying to myself that if it was not possible to make the oxen move more rapidly, there was danger of my dying, all of which was foolishness, even wickedness, as you will agree.

To force the beasts to a more rapid pace was absolutely impossible. Already the sheep as well as the oxen were showing signs of exhaustion and panting for water. Their tongues were hanging out, and they moved slowly as if unable to go farther, while five of the cows had dropped down on the trail as if dying.

We were forced to leave them behind, fearing lest if time was spent in trying to get the beasts on their feet again, more of the stock would fall.

I hardly knew how the remainder of that day passed, for I gave no heed to anything save my own suffering, thereby showing myself wick-

edly selfish, until a great shout went up from those who were in advance, telling that at last, after what seemed like many, many long hours, we had come within sight of a stream of water.

Then the oxen, wild with thirst and smelling the dampness in the air, plunged forward as if in a fury, for the drivers were unable to hold them in check.

In a mad race went every yoke of the cattle, drawing the heavy wagons that lurched first on one side and then on the other as we went over the uneven surface of the trail, until all the contents which had been stowed so carefully were thrown violently about, while we girls and mother had the greatest difficulty to save ourselves from being flung out.

QUENCHING OUR THIRST

The oxen continued on until every yoke of them stood in the creek, and there they halted, drinking eagerly until their sides swelled out as if bursting.

Regardless of the fact that our wagon was standing in not less than twelve inches of water, Ellen and I leaped out and drank from the stream like dogs, too thirsty to wait longer.

I have been in need of water many times since that day, but never have I suffered so keenly, and I now understand that the distress which well-nigh overcame me was caused for the most part by my foolishly

dwelling upon the lack of water, whereas if I had forced myself to think of other matters, much pain might have been avoided.

It was impossible to force the oxen across the creek, and we were obliged to make camp on the easterly side, for it seemed as if they would never have done with drinking.

When they were so full that it was impossible to swallow another mouthful, they refused to cross, but struggled to get among the rich grass which covered the bottom lands of the creek.

After the horses, as well as the men and the cattle, had been thus refreshed, half a dozen of our people, among whom was Eben Jordan, rode back on the trail, hoping to drive in some of the cows that had fallen by the wayside. It was not until a late hour in the evening that they returned, bringing with them only two of the animals.

Thus we suffered our first loss on the journey, and it seemed to me a most serious matter; but even before we had come to the trail which led to California, the loss of even twice as many cattle could not have disturbed me, for I had come to believe that we should arrive at that Land of Promise, if indeed we were so fortunate as to survive, almost empty-handed, owing to the difficulties of the way which the beasts could not overcome.

The next day's march was ended early in the afternoon, because then we had come to a stream, and those who were familiar with the trail knew we could not arrive at another place where water would be found until late in the night.

MAKING BUTTER

So we encamped early, and mother decided to set about churning, for long ago our store of butter had been exhausted. We had but a small quantity of cream, all of which had been saved since morning.

No sooner had she begun her work than fully half the women of the company followed her example, and at the side or in the rear of nearly every wagon was a churn set out with either the girls or the boys working the dasher.

As Eben Jordan said when he offered to spell me at the churn, it looked as if we people, who had set out from Ashley to find a new home in the land of California, had decided to abandon the idea and turn all our attention to making butter.

Next morning we were forced to continue the journey before having breakfast, for we were nearing the Kansas River, and would arrive there about noon if the march was begun as soon as daylight. Even then there would be hardly more than time before the sun set to get all our train over, for the stream was so deep that it could not be forded, and we must send the wagons across in boats.

A KANSAS FERRY

Although we were, as one might have supposed, in an uninhabited country, father told me that at this crossing of the Kansas River was a ferry owned by two half-breed Indians, who made a business of freighting heavy wagons across for a fee of one dollar each; but all the live stock would be forced to swim.

Now since none of the boats could carry more than one wagon at

a time, you may readily understand how many hours would be needed in order to get all our train from one side of the river to the other, even though it was no more than two hundred yards from bank to bank. Therefore, as I have said, it was necessary we arrive at the ferry at the earliest possible moment, lest night overtake us while half the company yet remained on the eastern shore.

The ferryboats were nothing more than square, shallow boxes, which the Indians pushed across by poles, after the cargo of wagons had been put on board.

Of course the women and the girls had nothing to do with this ferrying, save to remain under the wagon coverings where they would be out of the way. I envied Eben Jordan, who could move about at will, for verily my heart was in my mouth, so to speak, during all the time we were working our slow way across the stream, fearing lest our boat should sink beneath us.

THE SURPRISE AT SOLDIER CREEK

Not until nearly six o'clock were all our company on the western side of the river, and then I supposed that we would immediately make camp; but to my surprise word was given for the train to move on, and we journeyed three miles more, coming to the bank of Soldier Creek before darkness.

It was at this place that a most pleasant surprise awaited us. Colonel Russell's wife, who had walked ahead while our train was being ferried across the river, found quantities and quantities of wild strawberries near the camping place. As soon as we women and girls arrived, we set about gathering the berries, until each family had a good supply of the luscious fruit. Milk was not a poor substitute for cream to us who had been living upon corn bread and salt meat ever since we left the settlement of Independence.

During the next two days we traveled steadily onward, slowly, to be sure, but yet each step, as Ellen said again and again, was taking us nearer the end of the journey. In time I came to be impatient whenever a halt was called, so eager was I to have done with riding, for however comfortable a girl might make herself in one of the wagons, her limbs were certain to become cramped before night.

On the third day after crossing the Kansas River, the leaders of our company decided that a halt was needed in order to give the animals a rest. Their hoofs had become dry and cracked from traveling over the matted grass of last year, which covered the prairie even beneath the new crop, and it was necessary that something be done for them without delay.

I had been looking forward to a full day's halt, even though impatient when we were not moving forward, for Ellen and I had planned to wander as far from the encampment as we could, searching for flowers and wild peas, which grew there in great abundance, so we had been told.

BREAD MAKING

Mother decided that now had come a time when she must bake a plentiful supply of bread, for she was determined not to be put to such straits as we were during the rain storm, when it was next to impossible to build a fire in the stove, and, of course, I was glad to do whatever I might to aid her.

Before father had fairly got the stove out of the wagon and set up where it could be most conveniently used, nearly every other woman in the company had decided to follow mother's example, and then came such a scene as was presented when each family did its churning.

In the rear or at the side of nearly every wagon a stove was set up, and one might see everywhere women rolling or kneading dough, girls running about on errands, and boys doing their share by keeping the fires going.

I must say to Eben Jordan's credit that he was of great assistance to mother and me that day. If he had been a saint upon earth, he could not have done more or worked with greater patience than he did, running from stove to stove when the other boys had neglected their duties.

Mother told him laughingly that many times while we lived in Ashley she had been vexed because of the boyish pranks he played; but from this time onward she should remember what he had done in the way of aiding the cooks, and would overlook almost anything which mischief might prompt him to do.

PRAIRIE PEAS

The baking came to an end, so far as our family was concerned, shortly after noon; then Ellen and I, taking Eben with us as guide and protector, went out in search of peas and brought home enough to supply several families, who had been neighbors of ours, with a generous mess.

Save for the fact that these prairie peas look somewhat like those we have at home, I could find no likeness between the two varieties. The wild peas have a tough rind, and there are several seeds in the middle of

each; but after they have been boiled and allowed to remain in vinegar a few hours, they make a fairly pleasing dish.

When we began the march once more, I hoped to see the cattle moving more spiritedly than before the halt; but in this I was mistaken. It seemed to me that they limped painfully, and worse than ever; that I was not mistaken was proved, to my satisfaction at least, when I heard father and another man saying to each other that before many days we should be forced to kill two or three whose feet were in the worst condition.

However, the days went on and our cattle continued to work fairly well, although I noticed that when we came to rough places, such as the crossing of a stream, where it was necessary to climb a high bank on the opposite side, the drivers were forced to double up the teams more often than before, because the poor creatures could not haul so heavy a load as when we first started out.

EBEN AS A HUNTER

Within a week from the time of leaving Soldier Creek, Eben Jordan was indeed puffed up with pride. He came into camp late one afternoon dragging behind him an antelope which he had shot within two miles of where we halted an hour previous. This proof that he had shown himself a skillful hunter, caused the boy literally to swell with joy as he strutted around the body of the beautiful animal while our people were looking at it.

It seemed too bad to kill such an innocent creature as that antelope, and yet I forgot all the cruelty of it when Eben brought to our wagon enough steaks to provide all of us with a slice of fresh meat. Afterward it seemed to me much as if we had been cannibals when we so eagerly devoured the handsome animal.

From that day on, whenever we made camp before dark, Eben went out with his rifle, and more than once he brought in a deer of some kind, dividing the meat generously and fairly among us all.

A HERD OF BUFFALOES

Then came the time when we had our first glimpse of buffaloes, and never shall I forget the scene. We had been traveling in the bottom lands where we found multitudes of paths deeply cut into the ground, which some of our people said had been made by buffaloes; but we girls never so much as dreamed we might be near the beasts, until one morning father called me hurriedly to look out of the wagon.

Then I screamed, for we were literally surrounded by thousands upon thousands of those fierce-looking, yet stupid, beasts, who gave no more heed to our encampment than if they had been accustomed to such things all their lives.

They circled around within a quarter of a mile of where our cattle were feeding, and father said afterward that unless our men had been exceedingly watchful and active, the oxen and cows would have been stampeded beyond a doubt.

EXCITEMENT IN THE CAMP

Our animals were in a high state of excitement, striving to get through the lines of men who guarded them, and of course there was no possibility of our breaking camp until the buffaloes had departed, for, so father said, there was not a driver in the company who could handle half a dozen yoke of oxen while the buffaloes were so near.

Not all our people stood gazing stupidly at this sea of animals as did Ellen and I. You may be certain Eben Jordan was among the first to go out dangerously near the huge beasts, and he was followed by all the men of the company, save those who were guiding our live stock.

I had supposed that the buffaloes would take to their heels when a rifle was discharged; but much to my surprise they paid little or no attention at first to the reports of the firearms.

I dare not venture to say how many of the animals were killed; but certainly it seemed to me, when about noon the entire herd rushed off, the rumbling of their hoofs on the hard earth sounding like thunder, that there were no less than fifty carcasses spread out on the plain within a mile of where our wagons had been drawn up to form a corral.

A FEAST OF BUFFALO MEAT

There was so much game for us to bring in, that during the remainder of the day every man and boy that could be spared was kept busy at work skinning the dead buffaloes or cutting up the flesh.

What a feast we had that evening! We had buffalo tongues baked in the ovens, or in front of small fires which had been built here and there. Then there were what father called hump ribs, steaks, and meat

of every kind that could be taken from a buffalo. Each member of the company was eager to learn how every eatable portion of the animal tasted, and, therefore, cooked two or three times as much as could be used at one meal.

Our people had no more than time to skin and cut up the carcasses before dark; on the following morning word was passed around that each family must dry, or smoke-cure, as much of the flesh as possible within the next four and twenty hours.

Straightway every man, woman, and child set about either slicing the meat as thin as it could be cut with sharp knives, or putting together racks made of sticks, on which the strips of flesh were to be hung and exposed to the rays of the sun, as well as to the smoke of the fires that were to be built directly beneath them.

CURING THE MEAT

It was disagreeable work, and yet we were all, even to the smallest girl, content to do our part, knowing that we were thus laying up food for the future when it might not be possible to procure game, and when all the stores we had brought with us from Pike County had been eaten.

The arms of the men who acted as carvers were stained with blood to the elbows, while the hands and even the faces of the women and children who carried the sliced meat to hang it on the framework of sticks, were colored in the same way.

In addition to curing the meat in the sun and smoking it, some of the men made what is called pemmican, a most disagreeable looking mixture of flesh and fat which I afterward came to eat greedily, when we had nothing else with which to satisfy our hunger.

Pemmican is made by first drying the very thinnest of thin slices of meat in the sun, until they are so hard that it is possible to rub or pound them to a powder.

A bag is then formed of the buffalo skin, and into it is packed powdered meat sufficient to fill it considerably more than half full, after which tallow is melted and poured into the bag until it can hold no more. Then the entire mass is allowed to cool and harden. It is then fit for eating, so father said; but mother, when the time came that we were glad to have our portion of the stuff, always boiled it so it might be served hot.

It is not appetizing to me, and because I have seen the mixture prepared I can eat it only when I am very hungry.

A WASH DAY

Two full days were spent in curing the meat and making pemmican, and even then we did not continue the journey immediately, for the work had brought our clothing to such a condition that a day for washing was absolutely necessary. Therefore we remained for another twenty-four hours.

We were encamped near a small stream where could be had plenty

of water for the animals, and on either side of this tiny creek, shortly after sunrise, could be seen many fires, kettles, and washtubs.

What a tired girl I was when I stretched myself out on mother's feather bed in the wagon that night! It seemed to me that I had no more than closed my eyes before I was asleep, and not until father was bustling around inside the wagon next morning trying to build a fire in the cookstove, did I awake.

Then the patter, patter of rain on the wagon covering told that we were to be treated to another downpour of water, and eager though I was to reach California, I hoped most fervently we would remain in camp yet longer.

UNCOMFORTABLE TRAVELING

It was really difficult for me to open my eyes, so heavily did slumber weigh upon them, when I asked father if he had any idea of setting off in such a storm, at the same time reminding him how our beasts had struggled through the mud during the last rain.

He laughingly told me that we would continue on the trail, regardless of the weather; that a rain storm was not to be compared in the way of discomfort with snow. He said that unless we came to our journey's end before the season of frost set in, we might never arrive, but would be in danger of perishing, as others had who, striving to reach California, had been overtaken by winter among the mountains.

"So long as the cattle are in condition to push on, just so long shall we continue to march, regardless of whether the rain falls or the sun shines," he said, speaking very solemnly, and mother's face grew grave as if she was already beginning to understand the better what might be before us.

"There will be all too many days when we must remain in camp; but now, after such a long rest, it would be little less than wicked to remain idle here simply because it might be more to our comfort."

There is little need for me to explain how disagreeable it is to get up in the morning and attempt to keep a fire going with wet fuel.

Everything was damp and uncomfortable to the touch, and all the surroundings looked much as Ellen and I felt when we helped mother prepare breakfast.

After that very unsatisfactory meal

had been eaten, for we had nothing save some half-fried bacon with cold corn bread, not being able to make coffee because the fire would persist in going out, the train was started. Ellen and I, crouching in the rear end of the wagon where the rain could not drive in upon us, sat close to the stove, which now seemed warmer than when we were trying to cook breakfast, and talked of the future.

Of course I cannot set down all we said, for much of it was foolish; but some of the conversation I have remembered clearly even to this day.

ELLEN'S ADVICE REGARDING THE STORY

Ellen, when I had told her it was my intent to write the story of our coming from Pike County, said that it would not be proper for me to write anything about what we saw or did while on the Oregon trail. We were bound for California, and would not be upon the direct road to that country until we had left Fort Bridger.

It was her idea that I should begin the story with the time when we turned from the trail leading to Oregon, and set our faces directly toward California; but, as has been seen, I nearly forgot her advice, and even now it seems impossible to do exactly as she proposed.

I intend, however, in order to please her, to set down only such matters as seem to me of the greatest importance, and thereby hurry over a certain portion of the march, beginning in earnest with the time when we finally came to Fort Bridger.

INDIANS AND MOSQUITOES

Now you must bear in mind, although I may not speak of them again, that we were constantly meeting with Indians. Hardly a day passed that we did not come upon a village, meet a party of hunters, or receive visits from groups of two, three, or four who came to beg.

Strange though it may seem, we became accustomed to the savages

as one does to seeing a dog or a cat around the house, and gave little or no attention to them save when they made themselves disagreeable.

One other thing I will speak about now. Mosquitoes and tiny flies, which seemed as fierce as tigers, were with us all the time by day as well as by night.

When we first left Independence, it was difficult for me to sleep at night because of these insects, and during the day I spent the greater portion of my time striving to keep them off my hands or face. As the journey progressed it seemed as if they became less poisonous; but I suppose my body had become accustomed to the wounds, and I gave little heed to them except when the weather was exceedingly warm.

Until we came among the foothills, which is to say, after we left Fort Bridger, we found game in abundance. What had been sport to Eben became now a real labor, and he sought for fresh meat only when urged to do so by his father or some of us girls.

There were days when our men brought in no game because they were unable to come across any; but we were in a country abounding with deer, elks, buffaloes, and even bears, and so did not suffer for food.

PRAIRIE DOGS

Even though I say nothing more regarding the remainder of our journey over the Oregon trail, I must speak of the little prairie dogs which we came upon from time to time.

They live in villages, sometimes, as father has said, several acres in extent, and their houses are holes in the ground, with a top or extension, made of earth which they have pushed up from beneath.

Eben Jordan declares, and several men in the company who have talked with the trappers or hunters say, that in every prairie dog's house may be found a little gray owl, who has lodgings there, and oftentimes with this owl is a rattlesnake. Now just fancy the prairie dog, the owl, and the rattlesnake living together! All I ever saw of the family was the dog, and he is about the size of a large rat, with hair which is a mixture of light brown and black in color.

It is impossible for me to tell you how entertaining these little crea-

tures are. When we passed by the villages you could see them scampering around and barking. Again and again I have seen them playing about or sitting on the top of their houses, giving no heed to us until the wagon train was close upon them, when the entire colony would pop into their holes with every evidence of fear.

A moment later each little fellow would stick his head out, his black, beadlike eyes glistening, while he looked around as if asking whether or not you saw how quickly he could get under cover when it pleased him to do so.

I know of nothing more comical than these little animals, and yet they look so much like rats that I would greatly prefer to see them at a distance rather than make any attempt at taming them, as Eben Jordan declares is his intention to do as soon as he can catch one alive.

I have my doubts, however, about his being able to catch one, unless he is cruel enough to wound it first with a rifle ball.

COLONEL RUSSELL'S MISHAP

Just before we arrived at the Platte River, we crossed a small creek, the bottom of which was exceedingly soft; the men were forced to double up the teams in order to draw the heavy loads along, and Colonel Russell's wagon upset in midstream, where the water was two or three feet deep.

Now there was nothing comical in such a mishap, and yet Ellen and I, who were standing on the bank of the creek where we could see all that was going on, laughed until I felt actually ashamed of myself. It was all so ridiculous that I could not have kept my face straight whatever might have been the result.

If the accident had happened quickly, there would not have been anything so very funny about it; but, instead, the wagon toppled slowly, the men striving meanwhile to prevent it from going entirely over. In the heavy wagon were Mrs. Russell and four children. We saw first the youngest child, as if some one had tossed him out, come shooting from the wagon and strike the water. Then another child, and so on, one after another, exactly like a lot of grasshoppers, until Mrs. Russell herself appeared. Out they marched in the same order, water streaming from their clothing, which was bedaubed with mud.

Mother reproved Ellen and me severely for laughing when our neighbors were suffering; but even as she spoke the Russell procession passed along the edge of the bank, marking the way with mud and water, and I noticed that it was all she could do to keep her face straight while she scolded us.

CHIMNEY ROCK

When finally we crossed the Platte River, the men of the company rejoiced, although I was unable to learn why, except that it marked, as mother suggested, the first stage of the journey, the second of which would come to an end at Fort Bridger, and the third in that land where we hoped to settle.

Not long after crossing this river we had a first glimpse of that enormous mass which travelers speak of as Court House Rock, which, so those who have seen both say, looks from the distance not unlike the Capitol at Washington. A few miles farther on we saw another huge pile called Chimney Rock.

I doubt not but that both would have been well worth the seeing, yet our desire to look at them more closely was not gratified. The trail leads some distance off, and when mother proposed to father that we might halt for a day in order to get a nearer view of the curiosities, he shook his head decidedly, saying, almost gruffly, that we who were bent on finding new homes had no time to fritter away in looking at this odd thing or at that.

Eben Jordan, however, borrowing one of his father's horses, rode off

to Chimney Rock by himself, and when he came back he told Ellen and me that we need not shed many tears because of failing to see it close at hand, because it was nothing more than a lot of big stones that looked as if they might have been carelessly plastered together with mud.

Of course this couldn't be the fact; but Eben has no eye for scenery and, I dare say, might turn his nose up at what every one else would believe wonderful or full of beauty.

AT FORT LARAMIE

Forty-eight days after leaving Independence we came to Fort Laramie, which is more like a trading post than like a fortification. It stands on the banks of the river Platte, is owned by the American Fur Company, and is six hundred and seventy-two miles from Independence by the trail we came over.

Just fancy! We had traveled nearly seven hundred miles, the men of the company walking all the way; yet during that time, with the exception of the mishap to Colonel Russell's wagon and the loss of a few head of cattle, we had come to no harm.

At Fort Laramie we slept in a real house for the first time since

starting on the long journey. It was not such a building as we lived in at Ashley, and yet it was to me almost beautiful, after I had remained so long in the wagon.

I fancied I would sleep on that night as never before since the march began, and that we would have supper and breakfast properly and conveniently served.

I had supposed the mosquitoes and the midges were as thick in our wagons as it would be possible to find them anywhere; but when we came into that house the place was swarming with them, and they prevented us from closing our eyes in rest during the entire night. Never was a girl better pleased than I when the first light of day came in through the windows.

COOKING IN FRONT OF A FIREPLACE

After striving to cook food in front of one of the two fireplaces in that house, I was actually ashamed of having complained because our stove in the wagon on a stormy morning had seemed to me like some contrary animal.

However much trouble we might have had with wet fuel and lack of draft owing to the shortness of the stovepipe, it was as nothing compared with those rude fireplaces, where our faces were burned almost to a crisp, our eyes filled with smoke, and whatever was cooking came from the heat thickly incrusted with ashes.

I resolved not to grumble at anything we might find in California, provided we had conveniences where we could cook with some degree of comfort, and a place in which to lie down where we would be protected from insects.

TRAPPERS, HUNTERS, AND INDIANS

I suppose Eben might describe Fort Laramie so that it would to a stranger present the appearance of a stronghold; but for my part I saw there only scores upon scores of savages, loitering around outside the walls, gambling, racing horses, bartering furs, or gorging themselves with half-cooked meat, while here and there could be seen the noisy trappers, some dressed fancifully after the fashion of the Indians, and others decked out in buckskin clothing.

There were boasting hunters who swaggered around, peering curiously under our wagon covers when we had taken refuge there; and all

around, corralled or feeding near at hand, were cattle and ponies almost without number.

Our company was not the only party of Pikers at Fort Laramie. It seemed to me there must have been three or four hundred who had been traveling as we had traveled, some hoping to go into that land of Oregon which was represented as being wondrously beautiful, and others bound for California.

Ellen and I would have visited among the strange Pikers had it not been for the throngs of trappers, hunters, and Indians, such as I have already written about. Mother declared it would be well for us girls to stay in our wagon, and this she came to believe firmly after two of the trappers engaged in a downright battle wherein both used knives, and both were sorely wounded.

The people round about did not appear to think this fighting wicked or strange, and instead of endeavoring to make peace among them, all, even a few women, stood around watching the fray as if it was some exhibition of an innocent nature.

I was sick with the sights of Fort Laramie even before mother sent Ellen and me to the wagon, and felt well content to remain there until next morning, never grumbling when I struggled to keep a fire going in the stove in order that we might cook supper.

ON THE TRAIL ONCE MORE

It seemed to me that every member of our company, with the possible exception of Eben Jordan, was delighted when the word had been passed around during the evening that we should pull out at early daybreak.

We were getting near to that forking of the trail where we would bear southward and then westward, passing around a great salt sea on our way to California.

We soon came among the foothills, and it was really a relief to be climbing up one hill and sliding down another, instead of driving over a level plain where was nothing to vary the monotony. Although Ellen and I were pleased with this change in the appearance of the country, our fathers found little in it to give them pleasure, for we had come to where grass was scanty and the way difficult for the animals.

As father said, from then on we might suffer such privations and hardships as we had not experienced since leaving Independence; but that I could hardly credit, for it did not seem to me possible we would have more discomfort than when we were marching in the rain, with the ground so soft that the cattle could only with difficulty drag the wagon along.

I suppose our people did have some trouble in finding grass for the animals; but we girls knew little regarding such matters. Our work was to aid in preparing the meals, and, as Ellen said, in keeping our minds as cheerful as possible; these tasks we performed to the best of our ability, without hearing very much of the perplexities of the men, save when Eben Jordan came to us with tales of trouble.

INDEPENDENCE ROCK

After leaving Fort Laramie the first thing which particularly attracted my attention was a perfect mountain of rock, fully a hundred feet in height and more than a mile in circumference, father told me, which stood near the Sweetwater River, between the ranges of mountains which border the Sweetwater Valley.

It was an "imposing work of nature," so Colonel Russell said; but to me the most interesting thing about it was that the first celebration of the Fourth of July by a company of people bound to Oregon was held at the place. On the rocks, as high up as one can see, are a multitude of names, many, many hundreds, some painted, and others cut into the soft stone by those who had visited the place.

Another thing about Independence Rock which causes me to remember it even more than as "an imposing work of nature," was that near it one could pick up all the saleratus he needed, for there are veritable ponds of it, where, so father said, water filled with the salts had evaporated, leaving

the saleratus itself in pools which looked as if made of milk.

Next morning we came upon a great gap in the mountain wall which is called the Devil's Gate; through it flows a beautiful stream, on the banks of which we found wild currants and gooseberries in greatest abundance.

ARRIVAL AT FORT BRIDGER

About the middle of July we arrived at Fort Bridger, where we were to turn off upon the California trail, and where, if Ellen's advice had been followed, this story of mine would have begun.

Why it should be called *Fort* Bridger I fail to understand, for there are no signs of a fort about, but only three or four miserable log huts in which live two fur traders with their trappers and hunters.

One might have believed it quite an important place, however, because when we arrived there were no less than five hundred Indians of the Snake tribe encamped round about the log huts. Beyond them on every hand could be seen wagon train after wagon train of people who had come not only from Pike County, but from Ohio and Indiana, as well as from Illinois and Missouri, the greater number intent on gaining the Oregon country, with perhaps two hundred who were going to California.

Of course there were also at this place hunters and trappers, traders

coming from or going into Oregon or California, Spaniards, Negroes, and red men, the greater number of all this throng living in canvas tents, in wagons or log huts, while the rest made shift as best they might in the open air.

It was, like Fort Laramie, a place where Ellen and I had best remain in the wagons, for no one could tell what the savages might do if two girls wandered among their lodges, and certainly we had no desire to make their acquaintance.

Here, as everywhere since leaving Independence, we heard that song which by this time had grown threadbare,—

"My name it is Joe Bowers."

The Negroes and the Spaniards, the trappers and the hunters, were all singing it, and the wonder to Ellen and me was where so many people could have heard it.

WITH OUR FACES TOWARD CALIFORNIA

After spending one day at Fort Bridger we set off early in the morning with our faces turned toward California, and our hearts beating furiously. For the first time since leaving home it seemed as if we were really on the journey.

The trail ran up hill or down, all the way, but there was very little difference, so far as hardships were concerned, from that which we had already experienced.

During the first three or four days our fathers had no difficulty in finding grass and water in plenty for the cattle, although there were times, of course, when for mile after mile we passed through nothing but sage grass, which even the oxen would not eat. Every night during this time, we came upon a pleasant place in which to camp, and, best of all, so Eben Jordan thought, the game was abundant everywhere. When he had shot a small bear and brought it into camp, it seemed as if his cup of happiness was full. One might have thought the lad had performed some wondrous deed, from the way he strutted to and fro, repeating marvelous accounts of his battle with the beast.

AT BEAR RIVER

It was when we came to Bear River that I began to understand how different this trail was from the one which we had been traveling.

Instead of finding a safe ford, we came upon a swiftly running river, with a bed of rocks. So strong was the current that when father waded in to drive the oxen it was necessary for him to hold firmly to the bow of the foremost yoke lest he be thrown from his footing; the heavy cart pitched about until I was certain it would be overturned even as had Mrs. Russell's.

Mother said that if such an accident should befall us, it would be no more than a just punishment to Ellen and me because we had laughed so rudely when the Russell family were in trouble.

THE COMING OF WINTER

Two days after leaving Fort Bridger we had the first indication that winter was near at hand, even though it was then July. That night the buckets of water were crusted with ice a full half inch thick, and upon the tops of the mountains which towered so high above us snow had fallen.

You can well fancy how we shivered while making ready to cook breakfast. When the train had started, Ellen and I crawled under the bed clothing, for it seemed as if we were like to freeze, and no one knows how long we might have remained had not mother insisted that we should sit once more on the front seat, where we could see the wondrous beauties everywhere around us.

Just at that time we were traveling through what seemed to be a mountain gorge; towering many hundred feet above our heads on either side were crags which had been formed in the most comical figures. Some of them really looked like animals, and I could see now and then the head of an elephant or of a lion.

Later in the day father told us that we had passed in the early morning, while Ellen and I were asleep, a rock which looked so much like a beast that the trappers had given it the name of the Elephant's Statue.

During nearly two days we continued along these rocky roads, with the mountains overshadowing us, and in places the cliffs hanging so low that it seemed as if the rumbling of our wagons must cause them to fall upon our heads.

The next night we kept a fire in the cookstove because of the heavy frost in the air; then we came to a narrow pass between the mountains, where was a gorge or chasm, so deep that we could readily believe Eben Jordan when he said the people at Fort Bridger told him the sun never penetrated to the bottom.

It was what is known as Ogden's Hole, and got its name, according to one story, through being the death place of a trapper by the name of Ogden, who had hidden himself there from the Indians and was either killed by them or starved to death, Eben was not certain which.

UTAH INDIANS

There among the mountains we met a party of Utah Indians armed only with bows and arrows, and they journeyed with us until we camped for the night, counting as a matter of course upon our feeding them.

The Utahs looked to me more manly than any other Indians we had yet met. Surely they behaved themselves in a seemly manner, for when supper had been made ready, they seated themselves in a circle and waited decently to be invited to partake of food.

On the following morning, after we had traveled about two miles, we came upon mountains which looked as if they were standing there to bar our advance, and for the life of us neither Ellen nor I could understand how it would be possible to continue the journey.

Even the men of the company were perplexed, and during half an hour or more the entire train was halted while our people went first this way and then that, seeking some trail over which we could pass.

Then Colonel Russell came back to where we were waiting anxiously and said he saw a narrow trail winding directly up over those enormous cliffs. When he pointed it out to the other men, we girls overheard what he said, and I could not repress a cry of fear, for surely it did not seem as if any member of our company could climb to such a height, over so narrow a path, let alone trying to drive the oxen with the heavy carts.

A DANGEROUS TRAIL

However, there was nothing to be done save attempt the dangerous passage, unless, indeed, we were willing to turn our faces toward Fort Bridger, admitting we had been beaten.

My heart was literally in my mouth when we began that terrible climb among loose rocks, over a path so narrow that it seemed, if the

wheels of the wagon slipped ever so little, we would be hurled to the bottom of the cañon, which is another word for a deep valley or a rift in the rocks.

The ascent was so steep that when we started no less than twelve yoke of oxen were needed to each wagon, and there was a steady, upward scrambling climb of fully two miles; therefore you can well understand how many hours we spent in making that short portion of the journey.

Only one wagon was sent up the trail at a time, lest through some accident it should run backward and crush whatever might be in its path.

Until we were upon the side of the mountain where the trail pitched downward into the valley, I kept my eyes tightly closed, not daring to look at that dreadful depth into which the slightest mishap might plunge us.

When the panting oxen were brought to a standstill, the fearful labor having been performed, Ellen said that she had been so frightened she was actually exhausted, and indeed the perspiration, caused no doubt by fear, was streaming down her face when I ventured to open my eyes in order to look around.

I can conceive of nothing more horrifying than that journey, short

though it was in point of distance, yet so long while one was in a state of terror as to seem almost endless.

In going down on the other side, but one yoke of cattle was hitched to each wagon, and kept there only in order to hold the tongue steady and thus steer the huge cart, while the hind wheels were chained, so that, not being able to turn, they might act as a drag to prevent us from sliding swiftly to destruction.

Father said we had traveled no more than seven miles when we had crossed that terrible mountain. There we found ourselves in a valley green with grass, where ran a small brook which was most pleasing to look upon, since it told us that we would have water in abundance. Coming upon such a spot after so much horror, caused it to appear all the more beautiful.

SUNFLOWER SEEDS AND ANTELOPE STEW

Without knowing it at the moment of halting, we made camp near two Indian lodges, where lived ten or twelve of the Utah tribe; having gained so favorable an impression of those savages when some of the members had visited our camp, Ellen and I, with Eben Jordan, went among them, finding that they had set themselves up for traders, counting upon the settlers bound for the land of California, as customers. The women showed us a store of powder made from sunflower seeds, which had been parched and then pulverized; this they offered in exchange for food, or for ammunition. Ellen gave a loaf of corn bread for perhaps a quart of the stuff, and found it most agreeable to the taste.

That evening one of the men brought in a fat antelope, and mother made our portion into as savory a stew as I had eaten since we left Pike County. After that delicious meal and with the pleasing knowledge that we had come in safety over so terrible a road, I slept that night as soundly as I should have slept in my own bed at home.

It was decided that we would remain in that place, which mother called the Happy Valley, for a day, in order to give the cattle a long rest before they did more mountain climbing, and the housewives took advantage of the opportunity to wash clothing, bake bread, and do up such small chores as were necessary.

Consequently all the young people were busily engaged keeping the fires going, churning, or performing such other tasks as were required, so that we gave little heed to what was going on around us until, when the forenoon was about half spent, Eben Jordan excitedly called our attention to a huge column of smoke which was rising from the mountains to the westward.

A FOREST FIRE

At first I gave little heed to the matter, thinking it might betoken the location of some Indian village; but within another hour, so strong was the wind, the fire had been driven up over the summit of the huge mountain at the foot of which we were encamped, when straightway we had over our heads, as it were, a canopy of flame and smoke which shut out the light of day, causing it to appear as if night had come and the clouds were ablaze.

Half-burned leaves and ashes were scattered upon us until we were literally powdered as if with dust, and the men found it necessary to keep sharp watch over the coverings of the wagons, lest an ember should drop upon them.

During all the remainder of the day and until nearly morning, the fire raged with greatest fury; but, fortunately, the flames did not come down into the valley. When we set off next day, the cattle, much refreshed, went on at a swift pace; but the air was yet so full of smoke that my eyes ached, while the tears ran down my cheeks in tiny streams.

Our way now lay along the foot of the range of mountains which

sloped down to the marshy plains bordering that vast inland sea, which has always seemed so mysterious to me because of being salt.

THE GREAT SALT LAKE

It was about noon when we had our first view of the Great Salt Lake, and although I had never then seen an ocean, I could not believe the existence of anything more wondrous than that huge body of salt water among the mountains.

Father says the lake is probably a full hundred miles long, and at its widest part no less than sixty miles; but this he knows only from that which he heard from the hunters or trappers, therefore I am not setting it down as positive information. It seems to me I remember having read in one of my schoolbooks that it is no more than seventy-five miles long

and thirty miles wide.

However, this much which father says is true: that the lake has no outlet, and four barrels of its water being evaporated, will produce nearly a barrel of salt; therefore you can understand how much more salty it is than a real ocean.

No fish can live in it, and Eben Jordan declared that one of the trappers at Fort Bridger told him a man could not sink beneath the surface, so buoyant is the water.

The shore of this great inland sea was white with a crust of soda or salt, and the odor which came from the stagnant water in the marshes was so unpleasant as to cause me to feel really ill.

EBEN AS A FISHERMAN

It was on this night, when we had our first view of the Great Salt Lake, that Eben Jordan gave us a most pleasing surprise. We had halted quite early in the afternoon, and even before camp was made he disappeared; but I gave no heed to the matter when I heard his mother inquiring after him, for I thought the boy had gone off to try his skill as a hunter again.

Two or three hours later, however, it appeared that, instead of chasing deer or bears, he had turned fisherman for the time being, and when he came into camp just before we began to get supper, he had with him seventeen of the most beautiful trout you could imagine, which he had caught in one of the mountain streams.

They were so large that he literally staggered under the weight, and the single fish which he gave mother made an ample meal for all our family. It surely was delicious, and while eating it I made a mental resolve never again to speak impatiently or angrily to Eben, whatever he might do, for many times since our journey began he had been very kind to us all.

It really began to seem as if, after we had turned into the California trail, we were to come across everything which was strange and wonderful, for next day, after our train had rounded the base of one of the mountains, we came upon six or seven springs of water which was actually hot to the touch, as if on the point of boiling, and which smelled so strongly of sulphur that one would have been in danger of suffocation had the fumes been inhaled.

Those odd springs seemingly came up out of the solid rock, and mother, whose curiosity was so far aroused as to induce her to taste of the water, said it was bitter and most disagreeable; but she had no doubt it might be well for us all to take fairly strong doses by way of medicine.

GRASSHOPPER JAM

We were yet within sight of the Great Salt Lake when, one evening, three Indian men and two squaws, miserably clad and very ugly, came into camp bringing for sale or barter something that looked much like preserves.

Even though these people were so wretchedly dirty, I was hoping mother might be induced to buy some of their wares, so keenly did I hunger for something sweet; but I speedily lost all desire for anything

of the kind, when one of the men in the company explained what it was the Indians had for sale.

It seems impossible human beings could eat such things, and yet this man told me it was true that the Indians gathered a fruit called service berries, crushed them into jam and mixed the pulp with grasshoppers that had been dried over the fire and then pounded to a powder.

He called the stuff "Indian fruit cake," and, much to my disgust, not only bought a generous portion, paying for it with needles, powder, and bullets, but actually ate the mixture. I could not bring myself even to look upon it, after knowing what it really was.

Once more we came upon the mountains after leaving the shores of Great Salt Lake, and again we climbed up the steep ascents, with all the oxen toiling at a single wagon, and then slipped down on the opposite side, until it seemed certain some terrible accident must befall.

A DESERTED VILLAGE

One night we came to another place much like the one we had called the Happy Valley, and there we found an Indian village of fifteen or twenty lodges, every one deserted, although we knew the people could not be far away, for fires were burning brightly in front of the dwellings, dogs were barking, and many willow baskets filled with service berries were standing about.

It was a beautiful spot for a home, and I could almost have wished father would settle there, rather than continue on over a trail which was as dangerous as the one spread out before us.

There were in the valley poplar and pine trees with many willows, and here and there a patch of sunflowers shining out from the surrounding green with a golden glory.

I had supposed our people would camp there; but instead of doing so they continued on, planning to spend the night on the higher land.

When we were halfway up the ridge which led out from the valley, the Indians, whom we had evidently frightened, came out from their hiding places, whooping and shouting as if to scare us, although I saw no token that they were bent on doing us mischief.

We camped on a slope of the ridge, down which ran a small brook, and those who had tents set them up in a grove of cedar trees where they looked most inviting. When, however, Ellen and I strolled that way we found the mosquitoes and midges so thick that it seemed as if we had a veil in front of our faces.

That night the men of our company gathered apart from the women and children, seemingly to discuss some important matter; my curiosity was so far aroused that when I saw Eben Jordan I called upon him for an explanation, and he told me that we had come to the most dangerous part of our journey, where we must encounter perils so great that those which had already been overcome would seem as nothing.

THE GREAT SALT DESERT

We were near what is known as the Great Salt Desert; in fact, were to cross it on the morrow, and when Eben Jordan led me some distance farther up the ridge, I could see it at my feet.

The desert is covered with salt like sand, and on it grows nothing except wild sage, while from where we were then camped, until it would be possible again to find water, is no less than sixty miles, as Eben said.

Sixty miles over a soft surface where the animals would oftentimes sink fetlock-deep, and the wheels of the wagons plow into the salt sand until the progress must be woefully slow. In addition, all the while we would plod along knowing that no water was to be had, save what we carried with us, until the train gained the opposite side.

We were camped on the side of a mountain which seemed to be made up almost wholly of rock; this place had been decided upon because there could be found a small spring, yielding barely enough water to satisfy the desires of ourselves and the animals.

It was the last spring or stream of fresh water we should come upon until we had traveled across that desert, which, from the distance, looked like a great sea of milk. Once we had started upon the journey, it would be necessary to continue on, heeding not those who might fall by the way, so I heard father and Colonel Russell say, for the lives of our people depended upon our going steadily forward.

PREPARING FOR A DANGEROUS JOURNEY

Orders were given by the leaders of the party that our mothers cook no pemmican nor any salted food, lest it increase our thirst, and we ate bread with as much milk as could be had from the cows; within a few hours, for we were to set off again at midnight, another meal, consisting wholly of bread made from corn meal, would be served.

The water of the spring was so salty as to be almost undrinkable. During the evening the women and girls were busily engaged making coffee, for in such form the water was a trifle more palatable, and we were advised to fill with the coffee every vessel that would hold liquid.

As for the cattle, they would be forced to make the march of sixty miles with nothing to drink save what could be carried in two casks

which had been bought at Fort Bridger for that especial purpose.

When I asked father how it would be possible for us to give the animals drink even once, from no more than sixty gallons of water, he said they were not intending to allow the poor creatures to have what they wanted. The supply of water would be used simply to moisten the mouths of those that were suffering most severely. There could be no question whatsoever but that the live stock would be in great misery, and if it so chanced that we people escaped dire distress, then indeed we should hold ourselves fortunate.

BREAD AND COFFEE MAKING

Fortunately Ellen and I had little time in which to borrow trouble concerning the future, for every woman and girl found plenty with which to occupy her hands, as we prepared for the most dangerous and disagreeable portion of all the journey.

We made corn bread in abundance, cooking no less than three times as much as we could eat, for Colonel Russell suggested that it was possible we might abate the thirst of the animals by giving them bread in small quantities during the march, and so we filled every available place in the wagon with this food.

Mother made coffee enough to provide us with a supply on that night, as well as for breakfast, and, in addition, we had filled to the brim every vessel which was water-tight, until I should think we must have had no less than three gallons, while every other wagon was equally well supplied.

The men and boys were not idle while we baked the corn bread and made coffee. They had enough and plenty with which to occupy their time, for every piece of harness, every yoke bow, wheel, or other portion of the outfit which might give way, was looked after carefully, lest there be a delay, because a halt on the desert, so we had been told at Fort Bridger, might mean death to us all.

That night the animals were corralled inside our circle of wagons in order that they might be ready when the hour came for us to set off, and for the first time since I had known Eben Jordan I saw an expression of anxiety upon the lad's face.

Wherever one looked among our people he could see gloomy faces, and there was no more singing of "Joe Bowers," no whistling and joking among the lads, as was usually the case during an evening in camp.

BREAKING CAMP AT MIDNIGHT

When midnight came, I had a very good idea that there was more danger to be met in crossing the desert than I had been willing to believe, for we were awakened and told that the march would be begun in half an hour.

Father urged mother and us girls to eat and drink heartily while we might. When I asked him why we were to set off at such an unusual hour, he replied in a serious manner that from the moment we started until the desert had been crossed, there would be no halt made unless some of the oxen fell by the wayside and we were forced to delay in order to unyoke them.

When Ellen asked him how long a time the crossing would take, he said he hoped no more than twenty or twenty-four hours. He also told us it had been agreed that if one of the wagons should break down, or any accident happen, the unfortunate ones were to be left behind, the remainder of the company continuing on without making any effort to aid them.

Then, perhaps for the first time, I began to realize how much danger lay before us. Surely if our fathers had agreed that during the coming march they would make no halt for any reason, there must be grave cause for fear.

The men made ready for the march by the light of the moon, and there were yet no signs of the coming day when we set off; and then we were a mournful party indeed, the drivers urging their beasts to the utmost, as if they realized that every moment was precious.

THE APPROACH TO THE SALT DESERT

There was nothing very dreadful to be seen on the first six miles of the march, for then we were winding our way up the ridge, on the side of which we had been encamped, and save for the fact that Ellen and I were suffering from the cold, the journey was much the same as we had already known.

Then we rode down the other side of the ridge, among stunted cedar trees which looked as if they were dying from lack of water, and Eben Jordan came past our wagon to say we had come upon Captain Frémont's trail.

The fact that we were to follow in the footsteps of other human beings gave me more courage and caused Ellen to appear almost cheerful.

We crossed a valley where nothing was growing save wild sage, and then over rocky ridges which looked much like masses of dark green glass, through a narrow gap which might have been cut by the hand of man in the solid ledge, after which we saw spread out before us that vast desert plain, white as a sea of milk and most desolate and forbidding in appearance.

A PLAIN OF SALT

Not a vestige of any green thing could be seen within our range of vision. No bird was flying, and the silence was so like the silence of the tomb that I did not dare to speak aloud while calling mother's

attention to this thing or that, when we halted for a short time.

This was the last stop we would make, save in case of accident. Some of the animals ate the bread, others refused it, and then I saw what would have been, under other circumstances, a comical sight, for the men were going about with wet cloths moistening the mouths of the oxen.

After spending nearly an hour in making the final preparations, word was given for the train to set off. Instead of being like milk, we found that the desert was made up of a bluish clay, covered here and there in blotches with what was much like salt, and these white spots were so large and numerous as to give to the whole the appearance of milky white when seen from the distance.

The oxen sank fetlock-deep, and as we advanced there were times when they broke through what was like a crust, even to their very knees; therefore one can well fancy that the wheels plowed into this yielding surface until it was quite as much as the cattle could do to pull the wagons along.

LIKE A SEA OF FROZEN MILK

If all the way had been as difficult as the start, we might never have gained the other side; but as we advanced the surface grew harder and harder, until finally even the shoes of the horses failed to make any impression upon it. Then I heard father say, as he came back from time to time to speak with mother, that it appeared to him as if we were traveling over a solid crust of salt.

At the end of an hour, perhaps, we came upon what Ellen called another "soft spot," and for a distance of two or three miles the oxen strained and tugged at the yokes as they barely succeeded in drawing the wagons at a snail's pace.

Then we girls had most terrible forebodings, for it seemed certain we could never hope to cross that place before all the company had died from thirst.

To our great relief as well as the relief of the cattle, we came upon a hard surface once more, and the oxen were urged to their utmost speed in order to make up for the time we had lost while toiling through the salty dust.

There was no halting for dinner. Now and then we ate the corn bread, for with such terrible anxiety in our hearts none of us were conscious of hunger; but again and again and again did we sip the cold coffee, using it sparingly, however.

SALT DUST

It was nearly ten o'clock in the forenoon when a dark cloud began to gather in the south, and I said to mother, with great joy, that we would at least know the pleasure of being wet, even though we could not get all we wanted to drink, for surely there was a shower close upon us.

Indeed, we did have wind, with thunder and lightning, but not a drop of water fell. On the contrary, the breeze stirred up the dust from the plain and filled the air with it, and our parched throats grew yet more dry because of the salt which we were forced to inhale, even though we covered our faces with cloths.

How the poor beasts suffered! Their tongues were actually covered with salt, and not a mouthful of water could they have as a relief from their distress.

Save for the absence of rain, it was a veritable tempest of thunder and lightning, lasting about twenty minutes; then the sun came out with more heat, as it seemed to me, than before, which but served to increase our desire for water.

When the sun was no more than three hours from setting, I strained my eyes ahead, hoping to see the end of this horrible journey, although mother had told me there was no possibility of our coming to water until late in the night, and I saw the foremost of the wagons leaving the white plain, and passing over what promised to be a good road, toward a rocky range.

Then I shouted aloud in my joy, that we would soon come to where it would be possible to quench our thirst.

A BITTER DISAPPOINTMENT

For the moment mother believed I was right, but then Eben Jordan dampened our joy by telling us that we must ride over the ridge five or six miles, where were no signs of water, and then we would come upon another plain of salt, which was not less than twelve miles in width. Only after that had been crossed might we find ourselves in safety.

Ellen threw herself face downward upon the bed in the bottom of the wagon, and lay there as if in a fit of the sulks, while I crouched by

mother's side, wondering how long it would be before death came, for I had grown so foolish in my sufferings that it was as if life was nearly at an end.

COFFEE INSTEAD OF WATER

Mother left us to ourselves during half an hour or more, and then told us plainly that we were showing ourselves to be very foolish girls. She insisted that we eat the harder portions of the corn bread; that we take frequent drinks of the coffee, and, above all, that we resolutely calm our minds.

It must have been that amid all my distress I fell asleep, for suddenly I heard, as though coming from afar off, shouts of joy and the voices of men calling one to another.

Starting up, I asked mother what was happening, and gazed around wildly, for night had come and the moon was not yet risen.

"Thank God! the desert has been crossed, and we have come at last to where water may be obtained!" my mother cried fervently.

She leaped out of the wagon, we two girls following, and, running hurriedly, we went to where the men, boys, and animals had gathered in a group.

I believed we had come to a stream of sweet water, but it was only a narrow brook, where ran hardly more than a thread of water which had already been trampled upon by the animals until it was like liquid mud.

A SPRING OF SWEET WATER

At this moment Eben Jordan, taking Ellen and me by the hands, said, forcing us to run with him:—

"By following the stream to its head we shall surely come upon a spring."

And this we did, finding within two hundred yards a spring of the sweetest water I have ever taken into my mouth.

Ellen and I drank again and again, seemingly never to be satisfied, and it was only after I had shown myself very selfish that I remembered poor mother, who, most likely, was standing by that muddy stream waiting until the water had grown clear so she might drink.

Then Eben Jordan went back, and a few moments later returned, bringing with him all the women and children, and many of the men.

Having drunk our fill, Ellen and I went back to the wagon, where we ate heartily of corn bread, and then laid ourselves down to sleep, while the men and boys were bringing the teams into a circle to form a corral.

THE OASIS

After this we remained idle thirty-six hours, being forced to do so, as father said, because the animals were so nearly exhausted that a long time of rest was absolutely necessary.

It was during this time that Eben Jordan again displayed his skill as a hunter, for toward nightfall he brought in two small antelopes; but

the animals were so tiny that each family had no more than half enough to satisfy their craving for fresh meat, and we were forced to complete the meal with bacon.

Our halting place was on what can be described only as an oasis, stretching from that sea of white to the rocky cliffs beyond, and father told us that while we would not be forced to march over a plain of salt during the next day, the journey would be exceedingly wearisome and our suffering considerable, for another entire day must be spent without water.

Again we made preparations for a time of distress, by boiling more coffee and filling up the water casks with sweet water from the spring.

This time the anticipation was worse than the reality. On resuming the march, we traveled over the side of the barren ridge more than twelve miles, until we came to a well-defined wagon trail which, so some of our people said, had first been made by emigrants from Missouri.

I gave little heed as to who might first have passed over the trail, rejoicing with Ellen that at last we had come to some evidence of human beings; it seemed as if our troubles were well-nigh at an end, for we were told that this trail would lead us by the most direct course into that land of California where we hoped to find rest and comfort.

SEARCHING FOR WATER

From this on, during four wearisome days, we were kept upon a short allowance of water, and did not dare eat much food lest it should unduly excite our thirst.

Now and then we came upon a spring, when our water casks and every vessel that could be used for the purpose were filled to the brim, and yet again and again we suffered from thirst, but not so keenly as while crossing the desert.

Whenever I slept, it was to dream of the river we had left behind us on the border of Pike County, wishing that it might be possible for me to go to its banks once more, and, even though the water was muddy, drink my fill.

In due time we came to that point in the trail where we were forced to march directly over the face of the mountains. Here our fathers found the way so difficult that once more the teams were doubled up, twelve or fifteen yoke of cattle being put on one wagon, and, after hauling the heavy load to the summit of the range, driven back to get another.

Of course our progress was slow, and we traversed mile after mile only with severe labor on the part of the men and boys, for we girls and the women did no more than walk in order to lessen the load.

Then we came to a narrow passage amid the rocks, which was most frightful to look upon, although there was nothing whatever about it to cause alarm.

It was a gorge or cañon much like a tunnel, where the light from above was like a slender silver thread, and we went down into a narrow defile, where was barely room for the wagons to pass, and where the rocks, dark and fearsome, rose hundreds of feet above our heads.

THE BEAUTIFUL VALLEY

When we had passed through that forbidding place we received our reward, for we came into a most beautiful valley with water and grass in abundance, and, although it was yet early in the afternoon, there was no thought of anything save making camp, that we might enjoy the blessings which were spread out before us.

Before the sun had set Eben Jordan had killed another antelope; but he did not dare go far from the encampment in search of other game, for no sooner had twilight come than we could hear the howling of the wolves around us, until one's very blood ran cold. It seemed certain, and indeed was a fact, that we were literally surrounded by those ravenous animals, which were kept at a respectful distance only by the glare of our camp fires.

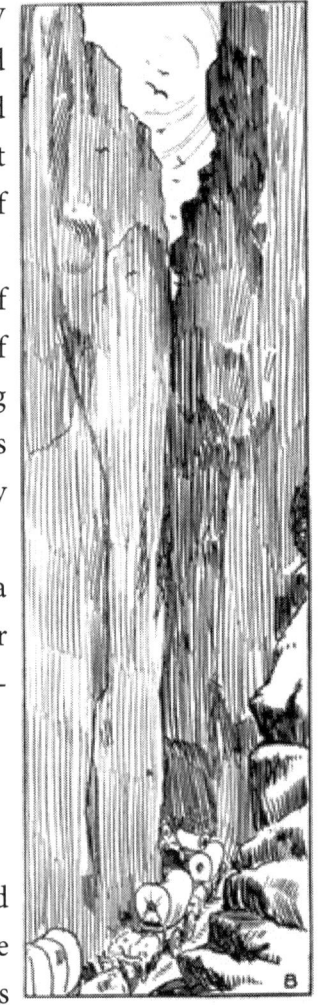

Next day, when we took up the line of march again, it was the same old story of climbing over rocky ridges and descending into valleys where could be found no signs of vegetation, until we had come to a very network of streams.

At our next camp we were visited by a party of Snake Indians, who, like the other savages we had seen, pressed around us, begging for bits of bread.

SNAKE INDIANS

Those Indians were not at all like any we had seen before; their clothing, what little there was of it, consisted mostly of rabbit skins

sewed together to form cloaks. To my mind they resembled more the Negroes than the Indians; but father said, save for their inclination to steal anything upon which they could lay their hands, that we need have no fear whatever regarding them, because they were known to be peaceable. The men were armed only with bows and arrows and seemed to have great fear of a gun or a pistol.

The visitors had with them a quantity of dried meat and roots which they wanted to trade with us for bread or for blankets; but our store of provisions was not so low that we would willingly eat what those creatures had prepared.

They lingered around the encampment, however, coming as closely to the wagons as our people would permit, and we girls and boys were told to keep careful watch lest they steal all our possessions.

Just at sunset, one of the men who was standing guard over the cows shouted that a wild beast was creeping up on us from a thicket a short distance away, to the right of where father's wagon stood.

Looking up quickly, I saw a huge panther crawling, as you might say, much as a cat approaches a mouse, and it seemed to me that he was making ready to spring directly upon us girls.

Ellen and I clambered shrieking into the wagon, where we hid our heads in a feather bed like the silly children we were, and straightway there ensued the greatest tumult that can be imagined, as our hunters strove to kill the ferocious animal.

It is, perhaps, needless for me to say that the panther escaped, although Eben Jordan claimed it would have been possible for him to kill the beast, had he not been hampered by frightened girls and men.

A SCARCITY OF FOOD

When the march was taken up once more, we journeyed over a less forbidding, although a not very pleasant, country, seeing antelopes at a distance, but so wild that even Eben Jordan strove in vain to bring one down.

During four or five days we marched westward, seeing now and then great numbers of animals which would have served to provide us with fresh meat, but our men were unable to kill any; then we found our supply of food growing so small that it was decided each person should have at a single meal no more than one slice of bacon and a piece of corn bread as big as a man's hand.

There is no good reason why I should set down such mournful details. While we were pressing steadily but painfully westward, so hungry that it seemed to me I could have eaten anything resembling food, and thirsty until my tongue was parched, the rays of the sun beat down upon us with pitiless fury, until we were so worn that life seemed at times like some frightful dream.

I can remember distinctly, however, what happened on that day when we heard those who were leading the train, shout that we had come upon water in abundance. When Ellen and I, leaping out of the wagon, ran forward, we saw before us several large springs from which the water was bubbling generously. Our delight was even as great as the disappointment was bitter, when the water was found to be almost boiling hot.

SPRINGS OF HOT WATER

It seems hardly possible that any liquid could come out of the earth so warm, and if I had never left Pike County I would have set down such a tale as a fable; but we did find boiling water, so hot that when Eben Jordan let down into one of those springs a slice of bacon tied to a string, it was well boiled in less than fifteen minutes.

However, we were not to be deprived of water even though it was hot, for father proposed that we fill some of our cups, declaring it would be sweet to the taste once it was cool.

This we did not only once, but three or four times, during the continuation of the march, for we came upon many of those hot springs on the trail after we left the banks of Mary's River.

Then came a day in August when, after an unusually wearisome

march, we suddenly overtook two emigrant wagons in which were fourteen people who had come from Missouri.

Verily it seemed as if old friends were meeting, for as our train came in sight, some of the strangers began to sing, "My name it is Joe Bowers," and however weary I had once been of hearing that tune, it now sounded in my ears like music.

That evening we spent visiting; those people, like ourselves, were traveling toward the land of California, and only those who have been journeying in the desert and through the wilderness, without meeting any human beings save Indians, can understand how intent was the pleasure we experienced in being with our own kind again.

The emigrants decided to join our train, and we were right glad to have them with us, although their store of provisions was no greater than ours; but all were put on what father called "short allowance," which was to each person two slices of bacon and two pieces of bread during one entire day. All our men who had guns were continually searching for game; but while we could see antelope and even wild fowl, both beasts and birds were so shy that the best hunters among us could not get within gunshot.

IN THE LAND OF PLENTY

And so we traveled on, hungry, thirsty, and weary, despairing now and then of ever coming again into a land of plenty, until we arrived at the Truckee River, which was more beautiful to my eyes than ever had been the broad Mississippi.

The waters of the river were clear as crystal and very cool, while from it our people took within an hour a sufficient number of trout to satisfy the hunger of all. It seemed necessary we should eat until it was absolutely impossible to swallow more, in order to atone in some way for the hunger that had pressed so sorely upon us during the ten days previous.

Eben Jordan said laughingly that we were much like the savages, who were starved one day and in danger of bursting with food the next.

THE TRUCKEE RIVER

It pleased me right well when father said that we were to remain in camp one full day by the side of this river, in order to give the animals the opportunity of feeding upon the rich grass which grew in abundance on every hand.

At last we had come into California, and a beautiful country indeed it appeared to me while we remained near the river,—all the more beautiful, perhaps, because of the suffering which it had cost us to get there. Both Ellen and I now came to believe our fathers had been wise indeed to leave the banks of the muddy Mississippi for so glorious a river as the Truckee.

All around us were evidences of bountiful nature, for the land was seemingly overcrowded with game, with food on every hand for the cattle, beautiful flowers, and everything which goes to make one happy.

How long the journey had been I did not really know until Eben

Jordan came to where Ellen and I were sitting on the grass with the skirts of our gowns filled with flowers. He had in his hands a bit of paper on which he had set down, from what had been told him by the leaders of the company, the distance we people had traveled since leaving Independence. This was no less than two thousand and ninety miles, to which one must add, in order to learn how long was our march, the distance from Pike County to Independence, which would, so Eben said, make a total of about two thousand two hundred.

Even then we were nearly two hundred miles from San Francisco; however it was not the intention of our fathers to journey so far across California, for we had not come expecting to find gold, but to make for ourselves farms, where we could live comfortably by honest industry.

Already I am writing as if we had come to an end of our journey, and so it seemed to me while we remained in camp on the bank of the Truckee River; but there were yet many days of toil before we arrived at the place where our people had decided to buy land.

It was yet necessary that we cross the Sierra Nevada, where we found a seemingly impassable trail over the mountains, yet we knew that people like ourselves, traveling in the same way, had gone before us, and all the dangers and the difficulties seemed lessened because of the fact that we had come so near to where we intended to make our new homes.

A HOME IN THE SACRAMENTO VALLEY

After much labor in descending the Sierras, we came upon the first settler's house we had seen since starting out. It stood in the valley of the Sacramento, on what is called Bear Creek, and was owned by Mr. Johnson, who himself was a Piker.

To me the house was odd looking, not because of being so small as to have only two rooms, but because it was built half of logs and half of adobes, or bricks of mud which have been dried in the sun. It was a rough building, and yet how homelike it appeared!

Unfortunately Mr. Johnson and his family were not at home. The building was closed, and although the door was not really locked, it had been fastened with strips of rawhide in such a manner as to show that the owner wished to keep out stragglers.

As we journeyed leisurely and comfortably down the valley of the Sacramento, we saw now and then large droves of wild horses and elks feeding

peacefully on the plains, and there was never a night when Eben Jordan, or some other of the hunters, did not bring in an abundance of game.

THE MISSION OF SAN JOSÉ

Then came that day when we arrived at the little village which is called the Mission of San José, and although everything about us was strange, we said to ourselves that at last we had come to our new home, for it was near that place our fathers intended to buy land.

The village of San José must at one time have had many hundred inhabitants; but when we arrived it was little better than a ruin. The houses, built of sun-dried bricks, were without roofs and crumbling slowly away, all of which appeared the more pitiful because of the well-kept church and the fortlike two-story house where lived the priests. Both buildings were in such good repair that they afforded a striking contrast to the tumble-down dwellings which could be seen near at hand.

I would love to tell how father built for himself a house on land which he bought from the priests of the Mission, and how mother and I set about making a home which should be somewhat the same in appearance as the one we had left in Pike County, but it is not for me to do so.

OUR HOME IN CALIFORNIA

It may be that at some time when our home here is fully made as we would have it, I can tell you how we live, what odd Spanish dishes we have on the table, how great a profusion of fruit is at our hand for the gathering, and very many other things which to me are most interesting.

I have learned to love this land even more than I did Pike County, which at one time I believed the most beautiful spot on earth, and although it pleases me now and then, when settlers come over the long trail, to hear the younger members of the company singing "My name it is Joe Bowers," I have almost forgotten that Missouri was once my home.

I have come to look upon myself as belonging to this beautiful valley where Nature is so lavish with all her gifts, and therefore, instead of calling myself a Piker, as in the days gone by, I dearly love to write so all may see, that I am now, and ever shall be as long as the good God allows me to remain in this world, Martha of California.

Made in the USA
Lexington, KY
11 February 2018